LEARN with Dr. Seuss

I Am Not Going to Read Any Words Today!

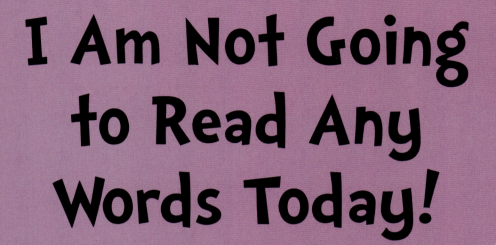

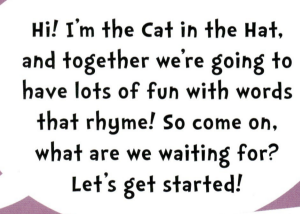

Hi! I'm the Cat in the Hat, and together we're going to have lots of fun with words that rhyme! So come on, what are we waiting for? Let's get started!

T0371151

HarperCollins *Children's Books*

The Cat in the Hat
™ & © Dr. Seuss Enterprises, L.P. 1957
All rights reserved
Published by arrangement with Random House Inc., New York, USA
First published in the United Kingdom in 1996
This paperback edition published in the United Kingdom by HarperCollins *Children's Books* in 2023
HarperCollins *Children's Books* is a division of HarperCollins*Publishers* Ltd
1 London Bridge Street, London SE1 9GF
www.harpercollins.co.uk
HarperCollins*Publishers*
1st Floor, Watermarque Building, Ringsend Road, Dublin 4, Ireland
1 3 5 7 9 10 8 6 4 2
978-0-00-859219-6
Printed and bound in China

First of all

there are some things
you should know.

I crossed it out.

 bit

I underlined it.

it bit

I said yes.

yes   no

I drew a line from here to there.

here ——————— there

PUP
BALL
CAT
BED
TREE
POP
HILL
BROWN

Read these words.

That's okay.
I'd rather play.
I am NOT going to read
any words today.

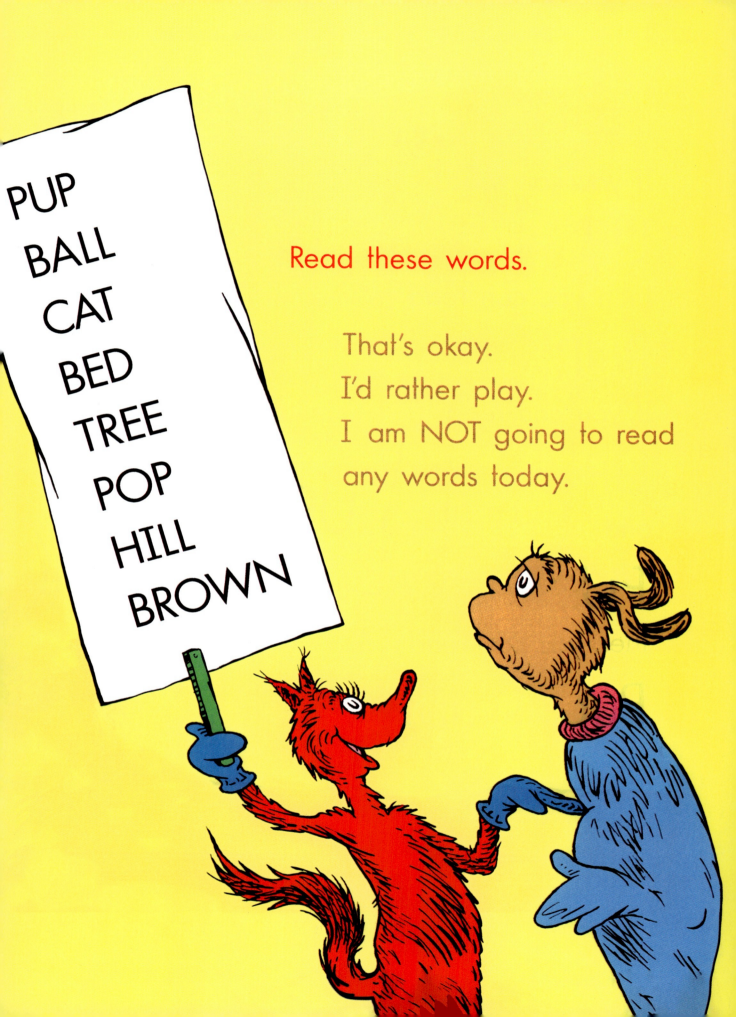

If you can read

UP,

then you can read

PUP.

If you can read

UP

and

PUP,

then you can read

Pup is up.

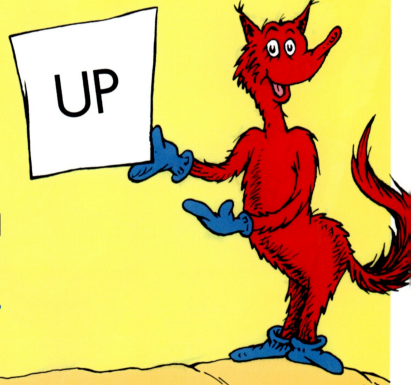

Pup is up.

[yes] [no]

Pup is down.

[yes] [no]

I say what I mean
and I mean what I say—
I am NOT going to read
any words today!

PUP
CUP

Pup in cup.

Cup on pup.

Pup on cup.

Cup on cup.

Underline the word cup.

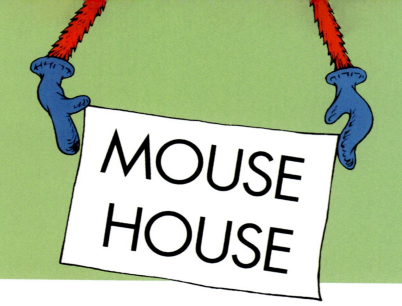

MOUSE HOUSE

Draw a line from the picture
to the words that tell about the picture.

Mouse on house.

House on mouse.

If you can read

ALL,

then you can read

TALL.

If you can read

TALL

and

ALL,

then you can read

We all are tall.

We all are tall.

We all are small.

We all play ball
up on the wall.

Underline all the all's.

The ball is small.

□ yes   □ no

The wall is tall.

□ yes   □ no

We play ball.

□ yes   □ no

We all fall.

□ yes   □ no

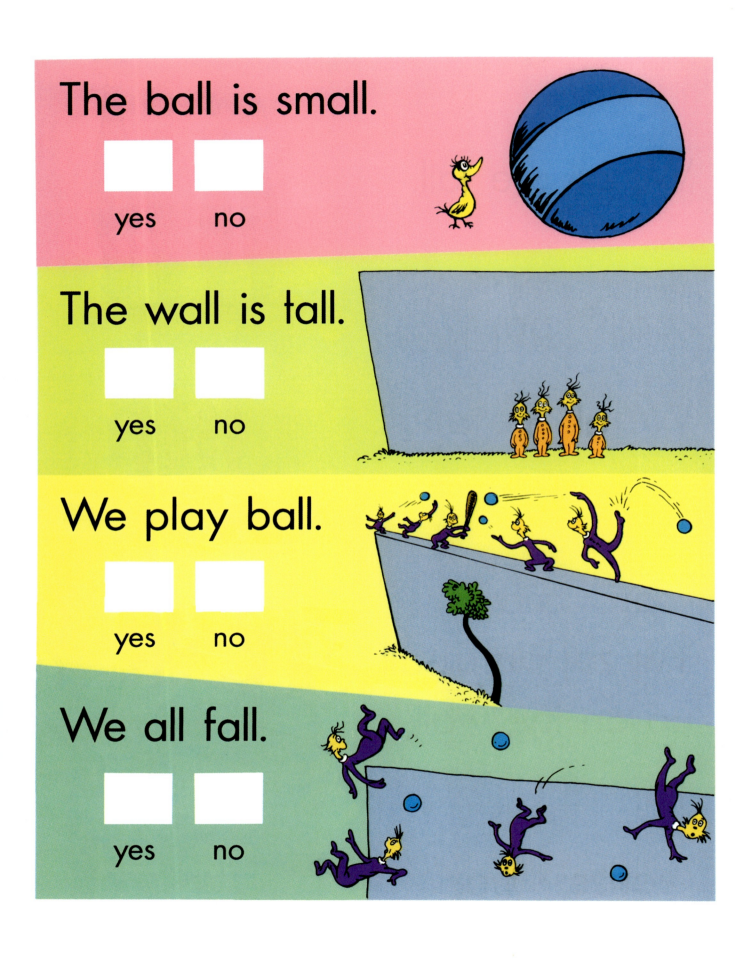

Pup is in the house.

☐ ☐
yes   no

Mouse is on the cup.

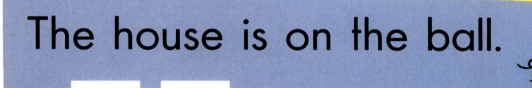

☐ ☐
yes   no

The house is on the ball.

☐ ☐
yes   no

The ball is on the wall.

☐ ☐
yes   no

Draw a line from the picture
to the words that tell about the picture.

We like to talk.

We like to walk.

SEE
BEE
THREE

We see a bee.

Now we see three.

Underline all the ee's.

Now we see three!
Please let me be!
I am NOT going to read
any words today!

If you can read

PAT,

then you can read

SAT.

If you can read

SAT

and

PAT,

then you can read

Pat sat.

Pat sat on a
house. hat.

Pat sat on a
cat. cup.

Pat sat on a
ball. bat.

Cross out the word that doesn't belong.

The house on the mouse.

Find the sticker that goes here.

The pup in the cup.

Find the sticker that goes here.

A wall and a ball.

Find the sticker that goes here.

A pup on a wall.

Find the sticker that goes here.

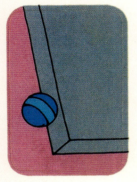

A SMALL SPECK OF FUN!

A BIG BLOB OF FUN!

FUNNER THAN FUN!

Good work!

Excellent!

Brilliant!

Good work!

Well done!

Hats off to you!

Hats off to you!

Fantastic!

Excellent!

Clever me!

Well done!

Good work!

Well done!

Brilliant!

Well done!

Clever me!

Good work!

Well done!

Clever me!

Excellent!

Three fish in a tree.

Three fish and a bee.

A ball and a bat.

The Cat in the Hat.

POP
HOP

We like to hop.

yes	no

We hop on Pop.

yes	no

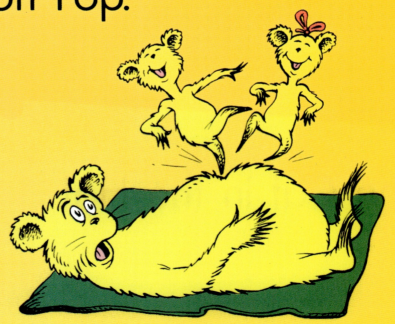

SING THING

That Thing can sing.

That Thing can hop.

Underline the word thing.

Things that sing!
Things that hop!
When is this stuff
going to stop?

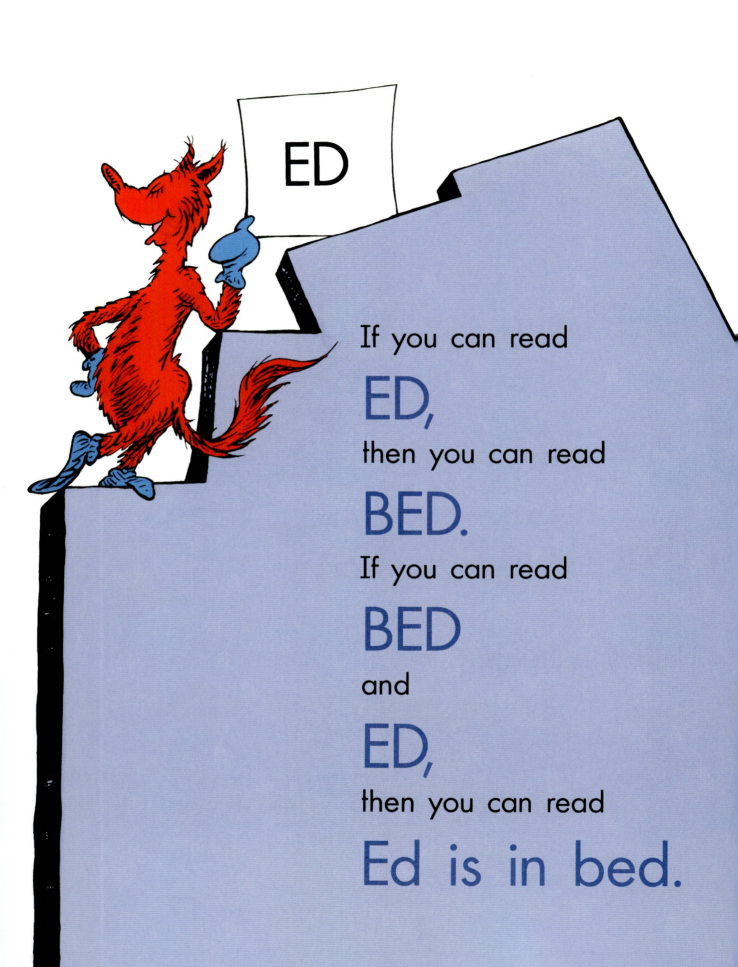

If you can read

ED,

then you can read

BED.

If you can read

BED

and

ED,

then you can read

Ed is in bed.

Red, Ned, Ted, and Ed in bed.

Underline all the ed's.
Colour the bed red.

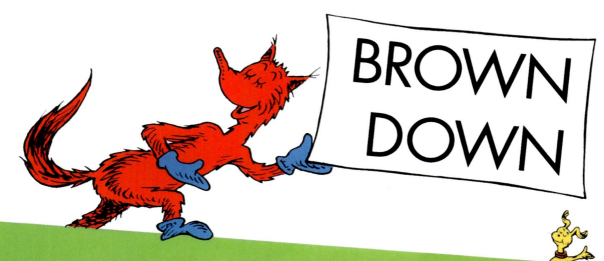

BROWN DOWN

Brown is
up. down.

Pup is
up. down.

Cross out the word that doesn't belong.

Who is Red?

Who is Brown?

Who is standing upside down?

Underline the answers.
Colour the dog brown.

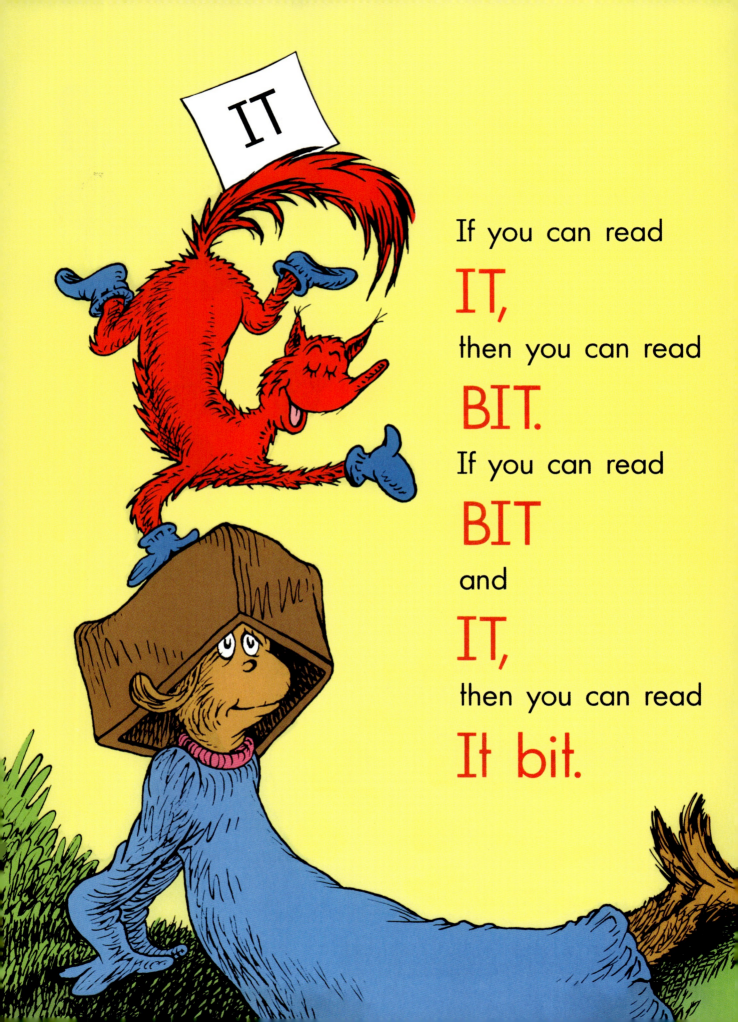

If you can read

IT,

then you can read

BIT.

If you can read

BIT

and

IT,

then you can read

It bit.

It bit.

We hit it.

We sit on it.

Underline all the it's.

A red Thing.

Find the sticker that goes here.

A brown Thing.

Find the sticker that goes here.

A tall Thing.

Find the sticker that goes here.

A small Thing.

Find the sticker that goes here.

A sad Thing.

Find the sticker that goes here.

A wet Thing.

Find the sticker that goes here.

A long Thing.

Find the sticker that goes here.

The wrong thing!

Find the sticker that goes here.

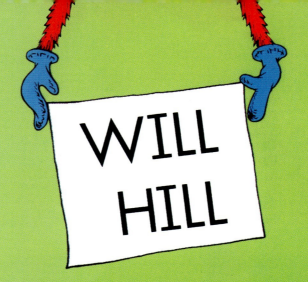

WILL
HILL

Draw a line from the picture
to the words that tell about the picture.

Will went
up hill.

Will went
down hill.

Will is still up.

☐ ☐
yes no

Brown is still down.

☐ ☐
yes no

Please let me be!
Please go away!
I am NOT going to read
any words today!

OTHER
MOTHER
BROTHER

This is my mother.

This is my brother.

This is my
other brother.

Underline all the other's.

Draw a line from the picture
to the words that tell about it.

They get wet.

They yelp
for help.

I am NOT going to read any words today!

I guess he means it.

yes   no

I am NOT going to read
any more today!
I read all the words.
I can now go away!
(signed) ....